1. We are here on THIS SIDE and you are there on the OTHER SIDE.

2. Between us is the HORIZON LINE.

3. You don't see we're here, on This Side, living our lives, because for you the HORIZON LINE is <u>always</u> <u>a day</u> <u>away</u>. You can walk for a thousand moons (or more for all I know), but you'll never reach it.

4. On the other paw, we know you're there because we visit you all the time. This is partly because of broomsticks. A broomstick has no trouble with any Horizon Line anywhere. A broomstick (with one or more of us upon it) just flies straight through.

And it has to be like that because scaring Otherside children into their wits is part of witches' work. In fact it is Number One on the Witches' Charter of Good Practice (see copy glued at the back).

On the other paw, it is NOWHERE in the Charter for a witch to go over to Your Side to make friends and try to be and do everything you are and do — <u>as my</u> <u>witch Haggy Aggy does</u>.

But then, that's my giant problem: being cat to a witch who doesn't want to be one. And as you will see from these diaries, it makes my life a right BAG OF HEDGEHOGS. So all I can say is, if HA tries to make friends with YOU, send her straight back to This Side with a spider in her ear.

Thank you,

Rumblewick Spel

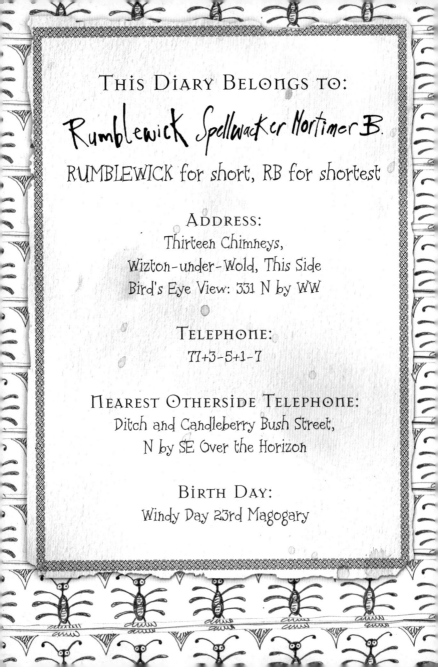

This Diary Belongs to:

Rumblewick Spellwacker Mortimer B.

RUMBLEWICK for short, RB for shortest

Address:
Thirteen Chimneys,
Wizton-under-Wold, This Side
Bird's Eye View: 331 N by WW

Telephone:
77+3-5+1-7

Nearest Otherside Telephone:
Ditch and Candleberry Bush Street,
N by SE Over the Horizon

Birth Day:
Windy Day 23rd Magogary

Education:
The Awethunder School For Familiars
12-Moon Apprenticeship to the
High Hag Witch Trixie Fiddlestick

Qualifications:
Certified Witch's Familiar

Current Employment:
Seven-year contract with Witch Hagatha Agatha,
Haggy Aggy for short, HA for shortest

Hobbies:
Catnastics, Point-to-Point Shrewing, Languages

Next of Kin:
Uncle Sherbet (retired Witch's Familiar)
Mouldy Old Cottage,
Flying Teapot Street,
Prancetown

Dear Diary,

Haggy Aggy has been sorting out her collection of headwear. She has tried on every hat she has and guess what? Suddenly NONE of them suits her.

"Not quite ME, RB, don't you agree?" she's been whooping, as she sends hats flying out of the window.

Or, "The me I was, RB, but not the me I am!"

Or, "This makes my nose look so grottleskew, I've a good mind to turn its maker into a bottle stop!"

Or, "How did I ever buy THIS grubspit creation! Had I left my eyes at home in the EYE JAR?"

Sadly, as a result, she is now shut in her room getting dressed to go Otherside shopping — for headwear that IS her as she is today and/or hasn't been 'made by a hatmaker with the taste of a bog rat and the style of a stick insect'. (Her words not mine.) I've been counting her cries of,

"Oh, this just looks grimgrubble!"

and she's now on her

thirteenth outfit!!

I've knocked and said, "Why don't you do what every other witch in witchdom does when they go Otherside shopping — wear your black and make yourself invisible when we get there?"

"Because I like to BLEND IN, RB," came her answer. "As you very well know. I like to be part of the hubb and bubb. To look and feel like one of THEM. And are you ready, by the way? Go and put on a pretty collar — with a proper

Otherside name on it."

Of course, that only sent me into
the slurrydumps.

It means I have to go Otherside
shopping with her. And I've so much to
do here — like trim the broomsticks and
get in some spiders. I mean look at this
place. She's been at it again
and it's just about WEBLESS.

SOCKS.

Someone or many ones — judging
by the sound — are knocking
at our door.
I'd better go and see
who they are.

Dear Diary,

All four High Hags — that's who came knocking.

They were each holding one of the hats HA had sent flying — which had apparently nearly knocked them off their broomsticks as they were passing. THEY WANTED A WORD WITH HER ON THE SUBJECT OF

'THE HAZARDS OF FLYING HEADWEAR'.

I told them HA was busy behind closed doors and not available for comment but they plumped themselves down on the sofa and said they'd wait until she was.

So, in order to drown out HA's very available comments about the outfits she was trying on, I turned on the TV.

It was showing an Otherside pre-historic beast show. The Hags were glued. They hooted and crawed. They hooped and tut-whitted. They marvelled as if they'd never seen anything like it before.

And then, when I questioned them
further, it turns out they haven't seen
anything like it before. It turns out there
isn't a single Otherside TV in the whole
of the High Hags' Headquarters!!
But now, having seen ours,

they were so eye-wacked,
they demanded to be informed
how to get one.

I was so amazed (as I thought everyone knew how), I just gabbled, "It's easy, your Hagships. Go to Stairrods Department Store on the Other Side and get one on your Shopalot Card. Bring it home. Plug it in. Press a few buttons and hey presto, it's all there. Simpler than magic. Though it is magic, I suppose, of the Simple Otherside Variety."

They were thrilled. "Very well, RB," announced Amuletta. "You will get us one by midnight and hey presto it for us. In return we will ignore Hagatha's

 overspending for this moon and not wait for her to come out from behind closed doors and be available for comment."

And off they trotted to their broomsticks and

flew away —
for once waving
approvingly down
at <u>me</u>!!

HA was <u>NOT</u> pleased when she finally emerged from her room — looking like a cloud of hedge-violets balanced on high white teeterers — and I told her of the unfortunate episode.

"Now we'll have to take the car in order to get their bladderwracky TV home. And I'm not in the mood for those Otherside parking masters who plaster our windows with sticky things and put turnstops on our wheels."

I promised to find us
a roof near the store to
park on — well out of reach
of the parking masters. And
I will. When necessary, I always do.

Anyway, got to go. She's already
in the car, hooting for me like
I've gone stone deaf or something.

After Midnight Of
A Grubspitty Grumbspewy Day

Dear Diary,

Just got back from delivering the High Hags
their Otherside TV. What I did NOT do was
hey presto it and make it work. For
very good reason as you'll soon
discover.

Meanwhile, to go on
from where I left off.

We got to town in no time

(HA put the car into
      express fly mode),

  and I <u>did</u> find us a roof to park on

        right next to Stairrods.

HA said I had to go and buychase the Hags' TV, as she wanted to get to the Hat Department without a tad of tell's delay.

I had to BEG on all fours for her to come with me as Othersiders do not take kindly to Familiars buychasing TVs with their witches' Shopalot Cards. (They usually get into a fright full froth and bother and call the Cat Catcher. And, according to my friend Grimey who experienced it once, being caught by a Cat Catcher and taken to Cat Prison is certainly not something to experience TWICE.)

Finally she agreed — but only AFTER we'd done her 'me as I am today' Hat Shopping.

22

Well, that took so long, the store was almost shutting by the time we got to the TV department. Furthermore she had almost no credit left on her Shopalot card and all we could get was a TV that had been 'reduced'.

(No doubt because it was so ugly nobody wanted to stare at it day and night.)

I wasn't sure the Hags would be happy but HA wasn't worried. "Like always likes like," she beamed, "and the ugly old Hags would want nothing else!"

She insisted it was carried to the car by a Stairrods' helper who did not seem used to cars parked on roofs and was very nervous about getting it up there.

"I didn't think," he panted as he humped and hauled, "it was possible to get a car onto a roof like this."

But HA just smiled sweetly and said, "Well, Helper, you learn something new every day." Then she rewarded him for his efforts with a lime green hat from one of her bulging hat boxes which made him run, as best he could on roof tiles, yelling,

"Stone staring mad!"

But here begins the First Really Grubspitty Part of this Otherside hat and TV shopping spree.

HA decided she was starving hungry.

"I have to eat NOW,
this tad of tell,"

she announced to the whole roof and those
staring out from some roof windows.
And then, almost falling off
the edge, she
spotted where
she wanted
to eat.

It was on the street below and called

THE GLITZERIA.

The outside was painted black and blue and covered in gold and silver stars like the night sky.

HA went into raptures. "That's the eatery for us, RB. A starry, starry place. Get out our foldaway broomstick — we'll leave the car here for convenience — and let us be hunger-answering AT ONCE."

I tried to talk sense into her as we flew.

I reminded her that witches NEVER eat on the Other Side as it is well known the food is grubspit.

"Old witches' tales!"

is all she snapped.

And before I could think of anything else
to stop her, she'd landed us, folded our
broom, tucked me under her arm like
Othersiders do with their unmentionables
(doglets) and was teetering into

The Glitzeria on her

high white teeter

Sorry Diary,

Fell asleep and dreamed I was being chased by agents of the High Hags —

Alien Wizards on Space Time Toads — until I fell off my broomstick only to find I'd lost <u>ALL</u> my ability to right myself mid air!!!

What a NIGHTSNAKE, is all I can say.

Anyway, where was I otherwise?

Oh yes, in a waking nightsnake under HA's arm in The Glitzeria with HA demanding the best table under the painted silvery moon on the painted night sky ceiling.

There was such a hush as we crossed the floor you could have heard a shooting star. Everyone was staring. EVERYONE.

The Outsider taking us to our table was polite but his eyebrows were nearly in the painted night sky.

He pulled out a chair for HA and she thanked him while giving him our folded broomstick to put in the umbrella stand. Then she said, flipping the name tag on my collar with a violet nail, "And a chair for Tiger here," meaning me.

The Outsider gasped.

"Madam, it is our policy that pets sit on the floor."

"But he isn't a pet, as such! He is my assistant who will read and decode your dish list," said HA. "Seat him here beside me. And give him one of these white nosekerchoo things to put on his lap."

The Outsider's eyebrows danced towards the painted moon.

He obeyed her though and soon I was sitting at the table doing my best to read her the dish list. (She did not go to Witch's Cat School like me and so does not read and write Otherside as well as I do.)

I was whispering so as not to draw attention to us but it didn't work. Attention was on us like we were at a Witches' Conference saying it is high time to stop scaring children into or out of their wits.

And anyway, unlike me, HA loved the attention and only wanted more.

In a loud voice, and smiling round at everyone, she chose five dishes (because she liked their names) and told the Eyebrow Dancer to bring them **all** at the same time.

I did not like the sound of anything and asked for a cup of comfrey which they did not have. So I ordered a herring without the pickle part as I thought we were in enough of a pickle without eating it too.

When all was finally laid out before us HA tasted each dish.

As she tasted her smiles and nods turned to frowns and glares. She went as white, green and puce as her salad — the first sign that a witch's fit is brewing.

And for once, I wished she would <u>NOT</u> be the witch she is and <u>NOT</u> throw a tempest.

My wishing didn't come true.

The fit was upon her and the rest of us.

"Hey you, with the dancing eyebrows," she yelled. "The Old Witches were right.

Who cheffed this GRUBSPIT?"

She got up, knocking over her silver chair.

"In fact," she screamed,

"where is this Grubspit Cheffer?

Take me to him or her or it.

Morning Early Of
A Guest Appearance. Day

Dear Diary,

Sorry — fell asleep mid-sentence AGAIN.
This time my shut-eye lasted till now,
which is early morning. And I've got to
feed the frogs, cheff up some sticky
catchfly pancakes for HA's breakfast
and — wait for it — get us ready
for a guest appearance on an
Otherside Celebrity Cheffing Show!!!

The frogs are tapping at the window but
I'll ignore them and go back to where I was
so you know the whole story.

And where was that? Oh yes.

In The Glitzeria, with HA demanding to see
the Grubspit Cheffer.

She pushed past the Eyebrow Dancer and teetered round opening every door until she found the kitchen — with me hard on her teetering heels trying to stop her.

I failed.

In the kitchen she started yelling at a Cheffer standing there with his hands in the air.

"GRUBSPIT AND GRUMBSPEW," she yelled.
"THAT'S WHAT THEY WERE.
THE FIVE DISHES YOU
SERVED ME.
WHY, MY CAT HERE
CAN CHEFF BETTER!"

The Cheffer who was clearly not the High Cheffer went red and called another Cheffer who clearly was.

AND HE WAS SMILING.

His eyes twinkled like real stars.

"Well, madam," he said, "if your CAT can cook better than we can, then please, be my guest."

He handed me a white apron and a white hat and bowed, saying,

"SO WHAT WILL CAT COOK FOR US?"

HA answered for me before I could speak for myself.

(Don't you just hate it when someone does that?)

"His Slime Buns are the best there are. Or so I am told. I try not to touch them myself as they're full of such dull magic. But his Ragwort Hot Pot with Pine Needle Salad. Now this is something else. This is lastcrumdishish in the tiptop of a tree extreme. This I adore. I could eat it every day of my lives.

Show them, RB...

uh...

I mean Tiger."

I looked round for
ingredients, my Lucky
Whisker drooping which is
a sign I am in deep quagmire.
(Which I was, even if I didn't
know HOW deep at that moment.)
Then — for an eye-blink — my
heart soared.

The High Cheffer said they had
no Ragwort or Pine Needles.

But it soon sank earthwards when HA
said, "The other supernova dish of his
which you haven't lived till you've tasted is
his Nuggets of Honeysuckle Stems
with Begone Berries. Not only
does it touch your mind
with ting and your
tongue with zingle,
it is also truly, truly
hunger-answering."

The High
Cheffer said they
had no ingredients for
that either which sent
my heart soaring again.

Though not for long.

HA demanded that he tell her what he DID have to cook with in this cavelet he called a kitchen. When the Head Cheffer had listed everything she yelled,

"WELL, NO WONDER YOUR FOOD IS GRUBSPIT! NO ONE COULD DO ANYTHING WITH THOSE INGREDIENTS!"

She ordered the no-longer smiling High Cheffer and his Undercheffers to clear the kitchen and leave us to it.

And then, I'm almost proud to tell, she did something only a great witch could do — which she is, of course, if only she were more willing. She pushed up her hedge-violet sleeves and turned everything in The Glitzeria's larder into proper cheffing ingredients!!

This is the spell she used:

THE GRUBSPIT-TO-LASTCRUMDISHISH-INGREDIENT SPELL

as invented on the spot by Witch Hagatha Agatha

All that's here upon these shelves
No doubt ashamed to be themselves
Tanging like old slosh and slurry
Chimney soot or skunkbed curry
All that's grottling to the tongue
Like eating washing not yet wrung
Or sitting here to lie in wait
And stage attack from on the plate
Insulting nose with grumbspew pong
And doing to the tumgut wrong...
Now on the count of thirteen fives
Each turns and magically contrives
To be what RB needs of it
Whatever RB now sees fit
Whatever dish he wants to make
The elements are his to take
He only has to wish the name
And it is here — the one, the same
No longer grubspit as before
BUT LASTCRUMDISHISH TO THE CORE!

And there it was — a larder overflowing with everything a cheffer such as I could desire.

I went into triple presto action because HA had said her cat could cook better than The Glitzeria's cheffers. If I didn't want us laughed out of the place — and I didn't — I had to deliver. So I put on the apron and hat and got cheffing:

First I made Fleabane Fingers with Mousemint and Crow Garlic in a Stitchwort Crust browned to perfection in some convenient sunbeams.

Next I wizzed up a Wig-You-Not and Teasel Lushti with a Mustard, Musk and Marsh Mallow Sauce — a dish I once made for the Hags when they condescended to come to a midnight breakfast. (They liked it so much they almost forgave me for letting HA come to the table in a pink dancing dress and silver headwear.)

When the dishes were ready, HA opened the kitchen door.

All the Eaterie guests, cheffers and servers including the Eyebrow Dancer were pressed against it and fell into the kitchen in a heap.

At once HA spelled them upright and shooed them out, only letting in the High Cheffer.

He went a tadpole green when he saw his larder, I can tell you, but he said nothing and began to taste — first the Fingers then the Lushti. And now

HIS eyebrows
danced.

He went "mmmm..." and "oh boy, oh boy, oh boy," and gobbled up every last smidgen.

His eyes spun thirteen times (as they should with these dishes), then settled into a glow and lit up the room with the inner magic I'd just cheffed him.

"There," said HA. "What did I tell you?"

He took a deep breath — AND THIS IS THE WORST OF IT WHICH I ADMIT I'VE TAKEN A LONG TIME TO GET TO BUT AT LAST HERE IT IS:

"Madam," he said, "I don't know who you are or how you trained this cat to cook if indeed it was the cat who cooked which I doubt. But here's the point. I have a TV programme called STARS GET COOKING. It features celebrities of every kind adding their special magic to everyday dishes.

Now, I would very much like you — with your cat if you insist — to make a guest appearance."

Well, since HA watches Otherside TV every tad of tell she can, just mention the words 'stars, celebrities, guest appearances' and there's only one word she will use in reply and she DID — thirteen times.

"YES! YES! YES! YES! YES! YES! YES! YES! YES! YES! YES! YES! YES," she cried, almost throwing her arms round the High Cheffer. "WHEN can we appear?"

He said, "Tomorrow," which sadly is now TODAY.

More when I can. The frogs are croaking up such a hungry din it'll wake the whole of Wizton if I don't go and feed them.

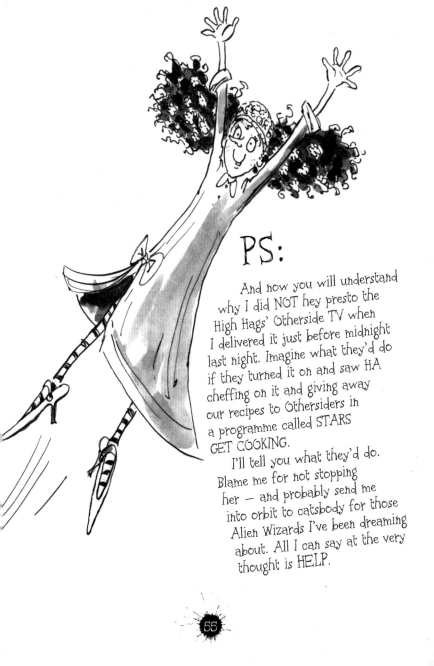

PS:

And now you will understand why I did NOT hey presto the High Hags' Otherside TV when I delivered it just before midnight last night. Imagine what they'd do if they turned it on and saw HA cheffing on it and giving away our recipes to Othersiders in a programme called STARS GET COOKING.

I'll tell you what they'd do. Blame me for not stopping her — and probably send me into orbit to catsbody for those Alien Wizards I've been dreaming about. All I can say at the very thought is HELP.

We Are Celebrity
Cheffers Day Night

Dear Diary,

BAD NEWS ON EVERY COUNT.

1 'Fizzby' (the name of The Glitzeria High Cheffer and first star of STARS GET COOKING as it turns out) was so pleased with our 'guest appearance' today he has asked us to appear 'regularly' which apparently means every day on every show.

2 The High Hags have left me thirty-nine reminders, by paw of their Familiars, to go over to their HQ and make their Otherside TV work. OR ELSE.

Here is the thirty-third reminder by way of example:

High Hags' HQ
The Peaks of Wizton-under-Wold
Of an hour close to dawning

Dear Rumblewick Spellwacker etc,

Fiddlestick, Underwood, Froggspittal and I, oneself, sit, twiddling our noses, staring at the otherwise attractive TV you brought us, but seeing nothing except itself. We ordered you to hey presto this machine so as to provide us with something tut-whitting and not-known-before to watch from the Other Side. This is our thirty-third warning that if you do not do what we ordered you may live to be VERY SORRY INDEED. And that means VERY, VERY SORRY INDEED.

Signed The First High Hag
Amuletta (Dame)

SO DO YOU SEE MY PROBLEM, Diary?

If I let Haggy Aggy do ① I can't ever do ②, namely turn on the Hags' TV. And if I do ② I can't ever ever let HA do ①, namely APPEAR EVERY DAY ON AN OTHERSIDE STARS GET COOKING SHOW — because without doubt if I've done ① the Hags will see her and I'll be for Alien Wizards' camp or worse — like back to Awethunder's to re-learn my lesson!!!

But the disastrous thing is — SHE'S ALREADY TOLD FIZZBY SHE WILL APPEAR. Which means I can't ever make the High Hags' Otherside TV work.

Which means I'm likely to end up being

VERY, VERY SORRY indeed.

So what AM I going to do? Get some peace and quiet to think straight for a start. Because I can't even think crooked here. I mean. I ask you. Just look at HA. In her 'appearance' on tomorrow's STARS GET COOKING, Fizzby has asked her to demonstrate how to 'add a little magic' to children's lunch boxes. And she's actually TRYING OUT RECIPES when normally she won't even boil a spider's egg!

She made me drag her bedroom mirror into the kitchen so she can see how she looks while she's doing it. And she keeps changing her outfit to match each new recipe — while talking to the mirror as if it is her 'darling Fizzers', as she likes to call him.

And in between she was saying things to me like, "I can never go back from this, RB — having Othersiders bow and scrape and give me starry clothes to wear and powder my nose and point cameras at me that transmit me straight to screen!

It's what I've always dreamed of. In comparison, being a witch is just GRIMROT and GRUMBSPEW."

Actually, I can't
stand being here
for another tad
of tell. I've got
to get out.

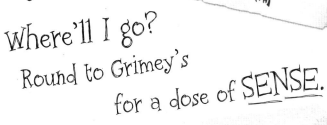

Where'll I go?
Round to Grimey's
for a dose of <u>SENSE</u>.

Dear Diary,

I've said it before. I'll say it again
a thousand times. Grimey is not my best
friend for nothing. He is the total moon of
total moons. Together we have come up
with <u>THE</u> <u>HOW</u> in: HOW to stop HA from
becoming what she isn't — a celebrity
cheffer easily seen on TV by the High
Hags — and save ME from being made to
be VERY, VERY, <u>VERY</u> sorry for the rest
of my life.

OH NO! HA's turned a tray of loosestrife
and figwort snackles into LIVE MICE with
two tails. That'll go down well on Otherside
school playgrounds — I DON'T THINK!!!

I'll have to go and sort it out. Tell you
about <u>THE</u> <u>HOW</u> of our plan when I can.

Dear Diary,

We did it.
Me and Grimey.

AND THIS IS HOW:

It involved disguise (which Grimey is always good at) and two large Ingredient Baskets.

It also involved Grimey's witch, Witch Understairs.

Understairs is a high witch in every way (lucky Grimey).

So high, in fact, it wouldn't surprise me
if one day she is elected a High Hag. She
takes proper witch's practice very seriously
and never fails for one tad of tell to
observe it to the last particle of the last
particular, usually over-properly.

She is full to bursting with deep
disapproval for Haggy Aggy's unwillingness
to be the witch she is and doesn't
understand Grimey's friendship with me.
(I think she fears he will catch her
unwillingness like a contagion by just
stepping through our front door.)

So — and this was all Grimey's brilliant thinking — we explained we needed her to help us save HA from bringing disgrace on herself and all of witchdom by becoming an Otherside celebrity cheffer.

And now she nearly burst with APPROVAL! And couldn't have been more eager to hear our plan or more willing to help put it into practice!

So with All In Place, we got up early this morning and Grimey came over to mine — already in disguise — the disguise of an Otherside Television Interviewer!!

I filled one of the two Ingredient Baskets for the show with (our own carefully planned) ingredients and the other with the disguised Grimey — and strapped the Baskets down on the back seat of the car.

Then, when HA had finally finished dressing, we set off in

express fly mode.

As soon as we drew up in the TV studio car park, I distracted HA by offering her a hand mirror I'd put under my seat — and 'suggested' she badly needed to check her hair and make-up.

While she fussed over that,
Grimey was out of his Basket
and off to 'borrow'
a microphone, camera
and some wires
to trail from them.

By the time HA was ready, so was he.

As she crossed the car park towards the Star's Entrance, he came rushing up.

"Excuse me," he said in a disguised voice sludgy with admiration, "you're the new star of STARS GET COOKING, aren't you?"

"I am," said HA. "And I'm fabulous."

"That you are," he said, "which is why I'm here asking you for an interview for the Intergalactic Channel. Everyone in every galaxy adores you and you really can't disappoint them."

HA was visibly torn.

I could see her thinking,

the Intergalactic Channel?

How giant is that?

At the same time, she was telling
Grimey she needed to get

'on set'

for her darling
Fizzby and
was already
running late.

Grimey assured her that
Fizzby would wait as long as
it took because he knew her
Intergalactic audience wouldn't. Then he
led her to a hidden corner of the car park
to keep her 'being interviewed' until I gave
him the signal he could stop.

At which point, dear Diary...and this
was the brilliant bit though I say it
myself...enter Witch Understairs...

disguised as

Haggy Aggy,

the guest star of

STARS GET COOKING!!!

We'd arranged for her to arrive by
broomstick close to the front of the Studio
building and away from the Car Park.

I wizzed out my foldaway and flew over to meet her and — even though I knew what to expect — nearly **fell off at the sight!**

She and Grimey had done such a good job spelling up her disguise even I could hardly tell the difference between her and the actual Haggy Aggy.

And when we went up to the Studio, Fizzby certainly couldn't. He gurgled all over us and sent us to be powdered and puffed.

Then he placed us in the kitchen that isn't really a kitchen (together with our Ingredient Basket) to start,

"ADDING A LITTLE MAGIC TO CHILDREN'S LUNCH BOXES!!"

And, as soon as the cameras began to 'roll', Understairs (as HA) was away, as if she'd been doing celebrity cheffing all her lives.

"Tangorango to you all!"

she crawed. "Into Thunderday's lunch box this is what we put. Two toad sandwiches — and these I prepared earlier. Thank you, Tiger."

I obliged from our Ingredient Basket!!

"Now,"

she showed the cameras.

"Always use sliced Slime Buns.

They keep the toads

fresh till 'opening' time."

Here she cackled like a klaxon.

Fizzby gasped. "You are joking of course. You mean two sandwiches containing... uh...avocado pear shaped like toads? Now, show us *how you moulded them?*"

"Avoh-ca-doh toads, I do NOT mean. They must be their living selves or where's the nutrition?" said Understairs/HA in a good impression of HA's voice when she's patronising grown Othersiders.

"Now, next in, to really spine-tingle the little ratlets you call children and wake up their brains...a packet of Hatching Spider Egg Snackles. Thank you, Tiger." (As I obliged again.)

"And in a moment I'll show you how to crisp them so they don't go soggy waiting for 'opening' time.

"And finally for the vitalities vitally needed by ratlets the world over, my favourite: Old Hornets' Nest Pancakes filled with freshly mashed caterpillars of the Hairy Stinging variety. And here, I'll show you how to mash them without getting stung..."

At this
Fizzby collapsed —

SPLATT — on the floor.

The live toads got loose. The hatching spiders hatched. The hairy stinging caterpillars fled before they were mashed.

The Cut Caller shouted <u>CUT</u>! (And a few other loud things I didn't understand.)

The cameras
stopped rolling.

And
Understairs, as HA,
was marched off
the set of the
kitchen that wasn't one.

I was cheering inwardly,
thinking,

WE'VE DONE IT!

Fizzers will never let HA near his
STARS GET COOKING show again.

And then I stopped cheering.

WHAT WAS THIS?

Grimey obviously couldn't keep HA talking to her non-existent Intergalactic fans any longer.

Here came

The One Thing We Hadn't Foreseen — the

REAL Haggy Aggy, flouncing in, calling

"Morning, Darlings,"

only to be met by a version of herself

(Understairs)

being marched out!!

For a moment, I was filled with dread that our plan had been skew-wacked. That now Understairs would be revealed for what she was. She'd be thrown out all right, for impostering as HA, but HA would be welcomed in! And we'd be right back where we started.

Luckily, there was no need to froth.

HA took one look at Understairs — the her that wasn't her — and was filled with a fright full fury suspecting she was trying to take her slot as guest star of

STARS GET COOKING!!

Well, talk about a witch's fit at the very idea.

She flashed thunder and lightning from eyes and nails. And everything in that television studio — cameras, camera workers, lights, light workers, The Cut Caller, the Cut Caller's helpers — SIZZLED, FIZZLED or just WENT UP IN A PUFF OF SMOKE.

And, in the fog, frazzle and smoulder, the HA that wasn't – Understairs – made a swift exit,

unnoticed

and

unseen.

So when Fizzers stirred on the floor and opened his eyes, there was only the real HA to see and blame. "I should have known," he spluttered, "from the start. You're not only a witch — you're a double witch! NOW GET OFF MY SET AND MY SHOW!"

As he fell back into his slump the Cut Caller (blackened with sizzle) marched HA out of the fizzled studio jabbering,

"AND NEVER YOU SET FFFOOT AGAIN HERE NEAR,

THE EITHER BOTH OF YOU!"

And that was the end of that. Or nearly. Back in the car park, HA was all for turning the false version of herself into an Otherside Ham Sandwich with An Unnatural Amount Of Mustard Inside It.

But, of course, she had no idea who
the imposter was or where to find her.
(And by now Understairs was Understairs
again and away with Grimey
on their broomstick.)

So instead, HA smashed the hand mirror
I'd handed her earlier 'for better luck' as
she put it. Then she bundled herself in
behind the wheel of our car, turned to me
and said, defiantly, "Well, anyway RB, who
wants to appear on a grumbspewy cooking
show with a cheffer called Fizzers who
doesn't know grubspit from a fleabane
finger? Not me. I'm way, way too much of
a star for that. Now come along home and
make me one of your lastcrumbdishish
Ragwort Hot Pots and Pine Needle
Salads. PLEASE!"

So I did. And though I say it myself, it truly was my best.

After that, I flew over to Hags' Headquarters and happily hey presto-ed their ugly Otherside TV, safe in the knowledge that they wouldn't be seeing us anywhere in it, on it or upon it.

Or not for the foreseeable tad of tell, at least!

WITCHES' CHARTER
OF GOOD PRACTICE

1. Scare at least one child on the **Other Side** into his or her wits – every day (excellent), once in seven days (good), once a moon (average), once in two moons (bad), once in a blue moon (failed).

2. Identify any fully-grown **Othersiders** who were not properly scared into their wits as children and **DO IT NOW**. (It is never too late for a grown Othersider to come to his or her senses.)

3. Invent a new spell useful for every purpose and every occasion in the **Witches' Calendar**. Ensure you or your Familiar commits it to a Spell Book before it is lost to the Realms of Forgetfulness for ever.

4. Keep a proper witch's house at all times – filled with dust and spiders' webs, mould and earwigs underthings and ensure the jars on your kitchen shelves are always alive with good spell ingredients.

5. Cackle a lot. Cackling can be heard far and wide and serves many purposes such as (i) alerting others to your terrifying presence (ii) sounding hideous and thereby comforting to your fellow witches.

6. Make sure your Familiar keeps your means of proper travel (broomsticks) in good trim and that one, either or both of you exercise them regularly.

7. Never fail to present yourself anywhere and everywhere in full witch's uniform (i.e. black everything and no ribbons upon your hat ever). Sleeping in uniform is recommended as a means of saving dressing time.

8. Keep your Familiar happy with a good supply of Comfrey and Slime Buns. Remember, behind every great witch is a well-fed Familiar.

9. At all times acknowledge the authority of your local High Hags. As their eyes can do 360 degrees and they know everything there is to know, it is always in your interests to make their wishes your commands.

CONTRACT OF SERVICE

between
WITCH HAGATHA AGATHA, Haggy Aggy for short, HA for shortest
of Thirteen Chimneys, Wizton-under-Wold

&

the Witch's Familiar,
RUMBLEWICK SPELLWACKER MORTIMER B, RB for short

It is hereby agreed that, come
FIRE, Brimstone, CAULDRONS overflowing
or ALIEN WIZARDS invading,
for the NEXT SEVEN YEARS
RB will serve HA,
obey her EVERY WHIM AND WORD and at all times assist her
in the ways of being a true and proper WITCH.

PAYMENT for services will be:
* a log basket to sleep in   * unlimited Slime Buns for breakfast
* free use of HA's broomsticks (outside of peak brooming hours)
* and a cracked mirror for luck.

PENALTY for failing in his duties will be decided on the whim of
THE HAGS ON HIGH.

SIGNED AND SEALED
this New Moon Day, 22nd of Remember

Haggy Aggy
....
Witch Hagatha Agatha

Rumblewick
....
Rumblewick Spellwacker Mortimer B

Trixie Fiddlestick

And witnessed by the High Hag, Trixie Fiddlestick

ORCHARD BOOKS

338 Euston Road, London NW1 3BH
Orchard Books Australia
Level 17/207 Kent Street, Sydney NSW 2000

ISBN: 978 1 84616 069 1

First published in 2007 by Orchard Books

A CIP catalogue record for this book is

available from the British Library.

Orchard Books is a division
of Hachette Children's Books

1 3 5 7 9 10 8 6 4 2
Printed in China/Hong Kong

To Catherine C, for
being supernova
H.O.

For Beatrice
S.W.

Dear Precious Children

The Publisher asked me to say something about these Diaries.
(As I do not write Otherside very well, I have dictated it to
the Publisher's Familiar/assistant. If she has not written it
down right, let me know and I'll turn her into a fat pumpkin.)

This is my message: I went to a lot of trouble to steal these
Diaries for you. And the Publisher gave me a lot of shoes in
exchange. If you do not read them the Publisher may want the
shoes back. So please, for my sake — the only witch in
witchdom who isn't willing to scare you for her own
entertainment — ENJOY THEM ALL.
Yours ever,

Haggy Aggy

Your fantabulous shoe-loving friend,
Hagatha Agatha (Haggy Aggy for short, HA for shortest) xx

ISBN 9781846160653

ISBN 9781846160691

ISBN 9781846160721

ISBN 9781846160714

ISBN 9781846160677

ISBN 9781846160660

ISBN 9781846160707

ISBN 9781846160684

Dragon's Bog

Dragon's Cave

The Narrow Avoid

BEYOND
WIZTON

CRAFTY CO-OP

OTHERSIDE

WIZTON